CLOWNS GONE BAD

A COULROPHOBIC ADULT COLORING BOOK

T0326175

FROM BESTSELLING
COLORING BOOK AUTHOR
M.G. ANTHONY

A PERMUTED PRESS BOOK

Clowns Gone Bad:
A Coulrophobic Adult Coloring Book
© 2017 Post Hill Press
All Rights Reserved

ISBN: 978-1-68261-348-1

PERMUTED
PRESS
Permuted Press, LLC
permutedpress.com

Published in the United States of America

More
COLORING BOOKS
to enjoy

AFTERLIVES
OF THE RICH AND FAMOUS
ISBN: 9781682611470
PRICE: $11.99

THE YOGA POSES
ADULT COLORING BOOK
ISBN: 9781682611302
PRICE: $11.99

HAMILTON: THE ADULT
COLORING BOOK
ISBN: 9781682612255
PRICE: $10.99

THE TAROT CARD
ADULT COLORING BOOK
ISBN: 9781682612644
PRICE: $15.99

THE TRUMP
COLORING BOOK
ISBN: 9781682610282
PRICE: $11.99